# TEXAS CAVALIER

# TEXAS CAVALIER

## The Story of James Butler Bonham

### By Rita Kerr

RIO HONDO JUNIOR HIGH SCHOOL LIBRARY

PANDA BOOKS ★ Austin, Texas

FIRST EDITION

Copyright © 1989
By Rita Kerr

Published in the United States of America
By Panda Books
An Imprint of Eakin Publications, Inc.
P.O. Drawer 90159   ★   Austin, TX 78709-0159

ALL RIGHTS RESERVED. No part of this book may be reproduced in any form without written permission from the publisher, except for brief passage included in a review appearing in a newspaper or magazine.

ISBN 0-89015-714-6

**Library of Congress Cataloging-in-Publication Data**

Kerr, Rita.
  Texas cavalier.

  Bibliography: p.
  Summary: A biography of the young lawyer from South Carolina who died at the Alamo after joining the Texans in their fight for freedom from Mexico.
    1. Bonham, James Butler, 1807–1836 — Juvenile literature. 2. Alamo (San Antonio, Texas) — Siege, 1836 — Biography — Juvenile literature. 3. Soldiers — Texas — Biography — Juvenile literature. 4. Heroes — Texas — Biography — Juvenile literature. [1. Bonham, James Butler, 1807–1836. 2. Soldiers. 3. Heroes. 4. Alamo (San Antonio, Texas) — Siege, 1836 — Biography] I. Title.

*This book is dedicated to those gallant men who died at the Alamo.*

# Contents

| | |
|---|---|
| Acknowledgments | vii |
| Introduction | ix |
| 1. A Boy in Red Banks | 1 |
| 2. Little Man of the House | 11 |
| 3. Off to College | 21 |
| 4. Rallying to the Cause | 30 |
| 5. The Alamo | 38 |
| 6. A Glimmer of Hope | 44 |
| 7. Darkness Creeps In | 50 |
| Epilogue | 59 |
| Bibliography | 61 |

# Acknowledgments

The author wishes to thank her many friends for their words of encouragement. Thanks goes to Joe Holbert, Shirley Wasaff, Ina Taylor, and Dwayne Willoughby and his family. Special thanks goes to a number of librarians including Peggy Summerlin of Coppell, Judy Encino of San Antonio, and Linda Reid of Killeen.

# Introduction

James Butler Bonham was born near Red Banks, South Carolina, on February 20, 1807. James grew up on the Bonham plantation and attended South Carolina College in 1824. He was admitted to the bar six years later and practiced law in Pendleton, South Carolina, before moving to Montgomery, Alabama. During the fall of 1835, James received a letter from his childhood friend, William Barret Travis, urging him to join Texans in their fight for freedom from Mexico. James traveled to Texas with the Mobile Grays of Alabama.

James's destiny — like that of some 188 other men — took him to the Alamo to fight against General Santa Anna and his Mexican army. James was twice sent as courier to request help from Col. James Fannin at Goliad. On his second trip, James returned after a five-day absence to find the Alamo surrounded and under heavy bombardment by Santa Anna's men. James courageously rejoined his friends in the Alamo, knowing that there was no hope of escape.

Three days later, on March 6, 1836, the Mexican soldiers made their final assault, which lasted about ninety minutes. Although the Texans' guns were silenced, their heroic stand gained them immortality. The words "Remember the Alamo" became the battle cry for Texas independence.

This book is based on these historical events.

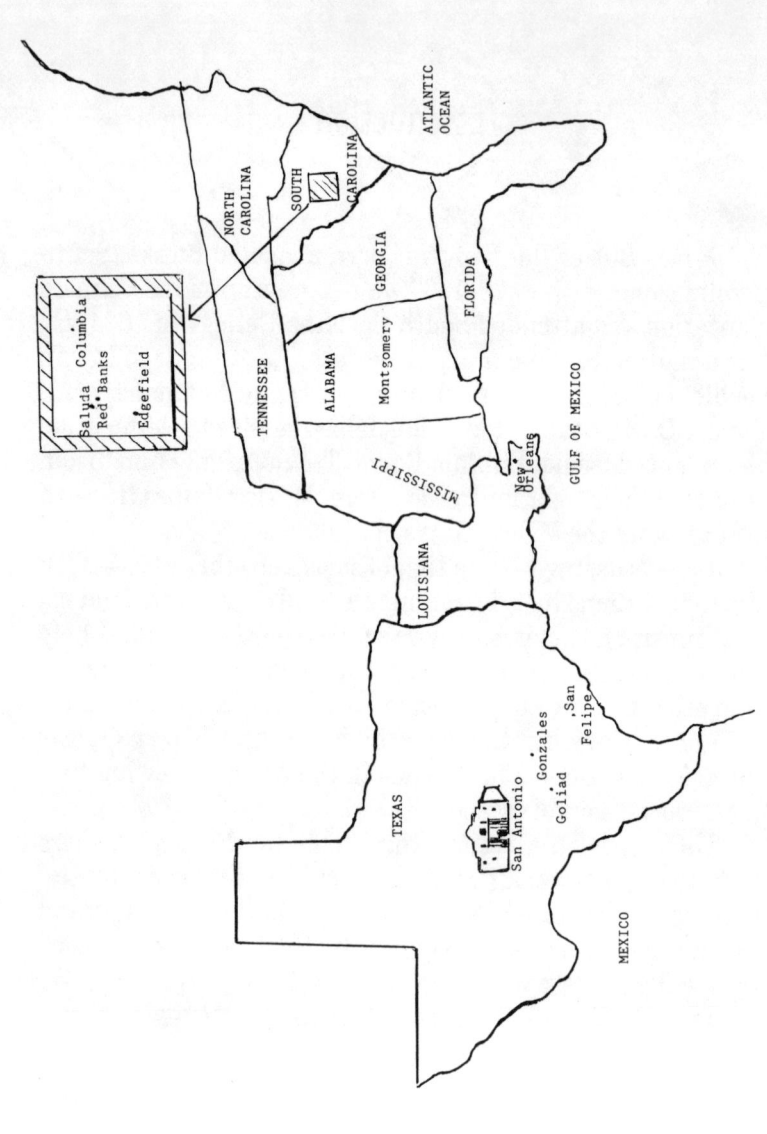

# 1

# A Boy in Red Banks

"I dare you!" The boy's angry face matched his red hair.

"Darers go first, William Barret Travis!" the taller boy screamed.

"But you know Ma would skin me alive, James Bonham, if I went swimming in Red Banks Creek before June."

"So? You want me to get in trouble, do you?" James cried.

"Well . . . no . . . but it's all your fault, James!" William stammered. "You were the one bragging you could swim better than me, just because you are two years older."

"It's true. I am older than you *and* Thomas. You're six and Thomas there is seven. You're just bigger than him, that's all."

William's blue eyes flashed angrily. "If you think you're so smart, why don't you go in swimming?"

"Whoa, Mister James," Thomas spoke up. "Don't you go in that muddy creek — not unless you want a whipping. If your mammy didn't whip you, my mammy would. You don't want that, do you?"

James wiggled his bare toes in the shallow water thoughtfully. The chilly water and Thomas's warning about a whipping helped him change his mind about going swimming. He said, "Well, I guess you're right, Thomas. Say, maybe we had better just catch crawfish."

"I reckon so," William agreed, bending down to peer under a rock. The idea of swimming was soon forgotten. The three boys busied themselves searching for crawfish. When one was captured, it waved two fierce-looking pincers in the air before it was dropped into a leather pouch that James had fastened to his belt.

The boys had lost track of time. Suddenly, Thomas raised his head and looked in the direction of the Bonham house. "Sh-h," he whispered. "Listen!"

They turned their heads toward the house and listened.

"James Bonham?"

"That's my mammy!" Thomas moaned. He knew she was not happy, from the tone of her voice. "Let's go!"

The boys forgot about crawfish. They raced to the black horse grazing nearby. James's long legs covered the distance quickly. He grabbed the reins as he threw his foot into the stirrup and leaped into the saddle. He bent over to pull William and Thomas up behind him. "Giddy-up, Blackie," James yelled excitedly. The horse picked her way up the muddy bank. When she reached the smooth path, she quickened her pace. "Don't make a sound. Let's surprise Aunt Tessie," James whispered when they neared the garden.

"James Butler Bonham? Where are you?"

The boys smothered their giggles with their hands.

"James Bonham?" The angry voice came from nearby. The boys made no sound. "James Butler Bonham — you had better answer me!"

The children peered through the leafy bushes and watched the woman lift the hem of her apron to wipe her perspiring face. When she finished, she straightened her shoulders and stomped her foot. "I'm not calling you again! I'm going to tell your mama, James Bonham!"

James's dark eyes twinkled mischievously as the trio emerged from behind the bushes. The woman stared angrily at

Aunt Tessie stomped her foot and said, "I'm not calling you again. I'm going to tell your mama, James Bonham."

the two larger boys and at her son, Thomas, as they sat on the horse's back.

"Aw, Auntie Tessie, can't you take a joke? We were coming."

Tessie put her hands on her thick waist as she watched the larger boys slide from the horse. James extended his hand to help Thomas to the ground. The boy slipped behind James in an attempt to escape his mother's eyes. He knew he was in trouble.

The warm rays of the Carolina sun beamed through the trees. The gentle breeze carried the voices of the workers in the rice field as they sang "Swing low, sweet chariot." Tessie was in no mood for songs. "This ain't the day for jokes, young man! You know your pa's not feeling well and your mama's busy fixing for your cousin's party. There's work to do. I've got no time for your foolishness."

James's sister walked into the garden before he could answer. Sarah gasped and threw up her hands in horror when she saw her brother. "James Bonham! You had better not let Mama see you looking like that!"

"What's wrong with me?" James demanded.

"Wrong? Just look at you. Why, I am ashamed to call you my brother! Your hair is a mess and you are covered with mud. Why, just look . . ." Sarah pointed to his feet. "The very idea! A Bonham barefoot in public! Where have you been anyway? Aunt Tessie's been calling you."

A grin spread over James's face. He reached into the pouch on his belt and pulled out one of the crawfish. "Look what I've got. Isn't it nice? It would look real pretty on your pink dress, Sarah. Wouldn't it, William?"

"Ee-e-e-e-k!" the girl squealed, turning on her heels. Her long, black curls danced up and down her back as she ran toward the house screaming, "Mama! Mama!"

James tried to hide his laughter by covering his face with his muddy hand. From Tessie's expression he dared not say a word.

"Now you've done it, young man! Get yourself in that washhouse this minute before I whip you myself!"

James pulled one of the crawfish from the pouch on his belt. He waved it at his sister saying, "This would look nice on your pink dress."

"Aw, Aunt Tessie," the boy pleaded pitifully.

"Now don't you start your whining!" She glanced in William's direction. "Mister William, I reckon you better get home before your pappy comes looking for you."

Young Travis rolled his eyes and started off on the run across the pasture as fast as his legs would go.

"I hope you don't get in trouble, William . . . See you at school on Monday!" James yelled after him. William did not stop to answer.

Thomas decided that it was a good time for him to disappear. His mother caught him by the ear before he could escape. "No, you don't! I'll take care of you later, young man. March . . . both of you . . . to the washhouse."

James moaned in protest, "Aw, Auntie Tessie, not in there."

"Hush your fussing. You get in there while I fetch the water. Thomas, you get the tub for his bath."

James groaned. Tessie's dark eyes flashed. "You don't think you're going in the big house with all that mud, do you? Now, you get those clothes off right now. I'll fetch one of your pa's big towels. You can cover yourself so you can run up the back steps to your room. Nobody's going to see you. Sakes alive, child, your sister is right. You are a disgrace to the family!"

Inside the large, two-storied colonial house, James's mother was making certain that everything was ready for the guests who would soon be arriving for the party. The delicate fragrance of gardenia and magnolia blossoms floated from the flower bowls on each table. The dark mahogany furniture sparkled like glass.

"Well, Lena, is everything about ready?"

"Yes, ma'am."

"How about in the kitchen?"

Lena nodded solemnly. "Tessie's got that under control, ma'am."

Sophia Bonham knew that Lena was proud of her daughter. Someday Tessie would take over her mother's duties of supervising the big house. Tessie's husband would someday be the overseer's helper, in charge of the workers in the fields. Each of the workers on the plantation had a job and was expected to do it. The cooks had to be able to load the table with mouth-watering delicacies at a moment's notice. Captain Bonham enjoyed entertaining. It was not unusual to have a house full of unexpected guests for a meal.

The captain, like many other Carolina plantation owners in the 1800s, delighted in horseracing and rooster fighting. Those sports gave the men an opportunity to bet and gamble. Sometimes, the captain's parties lasted for days. However, today's affair was to be a simple one with just a few guests.

Back in the washhouse, Tessie made sure that James was clean before she handed him the towel and shooed him to his room. He managed to reach his room without being seen. There he found that his party clothes had been laid out on the bed. James let the wet towel slip to the floor as he put on his soft white shirt. The delicate lace on the cuffs tickled his wrists. He wiggled into his undergarments and into his tight blue silk trousers. His socks fitted neatly over the pants just below his knees. After putting on his shiny black slippers, James grinned at the reflection in his mirror. His unruly curls were a mess. As he smoothed them down with his brush he got a glimpse of the mud under his fingernails. "Ma would see that for sure," he muttered to himself.

Thomas, who was waiting in the tree-lined drive in front of the house, did not look like the ragtag lad of a short time earlier. He now wore knee-length pants and a close-fitting blue waistcoat with gold buttons. As the first high-wheeled carriage came to a stop in front of him, Thomas grinned from ear to ear. The gentleman tossed him the reins and stepped down from the driver's seat. He offered the lady his hand and helped her from the carriage. After smoothing the ruffles of her billowy skirts of silk and lace, the lady placed her hand lightly upon the man's outstretched arm and they walked toward the house.

As the couple reached the door, it flew open. "Good evening, sir," Moses said, as he bowed. Moses had been the family butler for years. He had worked for Capt. James Bonham's father, Maj. Absolom Bonham, when the major served in the

Continental Army under George Washington. The job of butler was usually handed down from father to son. Moses felt certain that his little grandson, Thomas, would grow up and someday become the family butler.

Captain Bonham was kind to his workers. He treated them fairly. The captain made certain they had proper housing, food, and clothing, as well as medical care. Mrs. Bonham took an interest in the families to make sure that their homes were clean and comfortable. Because the captain treated them well, his workers respected him. They had heard him say, "Hunger and sickness breed discontent. No man can work on an empty stomach without complaining." He made sure that the workers had plenty to eat. They often ate ham, bacon, and sausage exactly like that served at the Bonham table. The Bonham servants took pride in Captain Bonham and his family.

Moses greeted the guests one by one. The final rays of sunlight were fading in the west when the last carriage arrived. Captain Bonham and his wife stood by the doorway of the parlor to greet their visitors. They introduced everyone to the guest of honor, the captain's cousin from Charleston. The oldest of the Bonhams' seven children, Sarah, stood near her parents. Sarah enjoyed her father's parties. She liked to watch the older people and hear them talk about her home.

The Bonham house contained many furnishings shipped from England. Among the prized items were two elaborately carved mantles above the enormous fireplaces at each end of the room. The men usually gathered around the fireplaces to talk. Most wore handsomely decorated waistcoats with lacy shirts. The women, in their elaborately colored gowns of silk and satin, blended with the rich surroundings of the parlor.

"Lipscomb, there you are. I was beginning to wonder about you," Captain Bonham exclaimed.

"Sorry we are late, but our son John decided to join us at the last minute. I hope you do not mind," the gray-haired man explained.

"We are delighted you could come. You remember our daughter Sarah? And this is my cousin, R. G. Bonham of

Charleston. It is good to see you, too, Mrs. Lipscomb." The captain lifted her gloved hand and, following the custom of the day, brushed the back of her hand with his lips. The captain looked up in time to see John Lipscomb speaking to Sarah. The girl was blushing. Captain Bonham wondered what the young man had said. Sarah looked especially pretty. The tiny bodice of her long, flowing dress emphasized her slender waist. At fifteen, Sarah was a true southern belle.

"Sophia," the captain whispered softly to his wife, "shouldn't the children greet our guests before we dine?"

"Yes, dear," Sophia said, giving the velvet bell-pull a gentle tug. At this signal, Lena entered the room carrying the Bonham baby in her arms. Three older Bonham children were by her side. A hush fell upon the guests as they turned to look at the children. The children all had their father's dark flashing eyes, black wavy hair, and olive complexion, and their mother's upturned nose.

The captain smiled proudly as he said, "Friends. Have you met our oldest daughter, Sarah?"

Sarah lowered her eyes and curtsied politely.

Captain Bonham realized that young Lipscomb was watching his daughter with special interest. He continued. "I regret that our two older boys, Simeon and Malachi, are still away in law school."

One of the older men whispered to a friend on his right, "Simeon and Malachi are fine boys. They will make good lawyers."

The captain went on. "This is Elizabeth, and this is Julia Ann."

The two younger girls curtsied sweetly.

"And this is our son James," the captain said proudly.

Mrs. Lipscomb whispered loudly, "He looks just like his father! Isn't he precious?"

James felt the blood creep up his neck. His face turned red.

"And this is our youngest son, Milledge."

The dimpled baby squealed in delight as he reached his chubby arms toward his father. There was little doubt that Captain Bonham was proud of his children.

It was a happy time. No one could foresee the disaster that would befall the family within a few weeks. Capt. James Bonham would soon be gone.

# 2

# Little Man of the House

A soft rain fell silently on the small figure standing by the new grave.

"Why?" James sobbed uncontrollably. "Why my father?"

There was no answer save for the gentle rain and the rustling of the wind through the large magnolia trees surrounding the lonely cemetery. The air was heavy with the haunting fragrance of the mountain laurel and dogwood blossoms.

James stared at the cold marble gravemarkers in front of him. Two bore the names of Capt. Jacob Smith and Sallie Butler Smith. They had been his mother's parents. The name on the smaller marker was Jacob Bonham. James's little brother had been only four years old when he died. And now there was a new grave. Capt. James Bonham was dead.

It had been a difficult day for James. The eight-year-old had tried to hide his tears during the funeral service. The hardest part of the service was at the end, when Moses and the other servants began their mournful singing. Some well-meaning person had told James that he would have to be the man of the house. But now, alone at his father's grave, James did not feel like a man. He felt like a little boy who longed for his father.

James was so absorbed in his grief that he did not hear his mother approach. She took him in her arms and crooned tenderly, "Oh, James, my little James." He buried his head against her bosom and sobbed. "Son, I am sorry — sorry for you and sorry for me. I just can't believe he is gone. How could it happen so quickly?"

The tiny drops of rain mingled with their tears as mother and son cried together. Finally, Sophia Bonham dried her eyes and looked heavenward. "Son," she muttered hoarsely, "look!"

A single ray of sunlight had broken through the heavy clouds. It was shining on the small clump of dogwood blossoms that James had placed beside his father's grave.

James wiped his eyes on his sleeve. He whispered softly, "Mama, do you think that is a sign we should stop crying?"

His mother nodded her head slowly. "Yes, perhaps your father is telling us to go on living . . . for him."

James swallowed the lump in his throat. "Mama, I want to be a good boy . . ." his voice faltered, "but I will need help. Will you help me?"

"Why don't we both pray for help? Nothing is impossible with prayer, son."


That afternoon in 1815, James Butler Bonham began a new phase of his life. In the days and weeks that followed, James tried to mend his ways. Everyone was amazed. Even his teacher was surprised at the change in him. He knew that James was an intelligent lad. But James had earned a reputation of being a tease and mischief-maker at school. His legs had been switched and his knuckles rapped more than once.

Most of the students in the one-room schoolhouse that James attended were boys. Many of the wealthier families sent their sons to boarding schools to get an education. Some parents felt that it was a waste of money to send their daughters to school. As a result, some of the more privileged young ladies studied music, dancing, and manners at home. Girls were taught the art of embroidery and needlework at an early age. Women were expected to busy their fingers with quilting or knitting and spinning. However, the two younger Bonham girls went to school with their brother. Elizabeth and Julia Ann were often the only females in the log schoolhouse, and were frequently the target for James's teasing. He delighted in pulling their long curls while the other students recited their multiplication tables. More than once, the teacher stopped the class to give James a whack across his tight-fitting breeches.

James's misbehavior had always been a source of irritation to the teacher. He never knew what the boy would do next. There had been that dreadful day before Captain Bonham's death, when the schoolmaster had threatened to resign.

The morning of that unforgettable day had been calm enough. The only disturbance occurred when James jiggled the bench he shared with the other students. The movement had caused them to spatter ink on their work. After a scolding, James had meekly resumed his studies. It was like a lull before the storm that was to come that afternoon.

At noon the pupils had taken their lunch pails out under the shade trees. While they ate, the schoolmaster remained inside, enjoying the peace and quiet. After the children had finished eating, they played hide-and-seek — all but James and the boy they called F.W. Although James and F.W. were not the best of friends, they were frequently in trouble together.

The two boys had headed for a wooded area bordering the schoolyard. F.W. saw a frog and managed to capture the creature. He stuffed it into his lunch pail. James chanced upon a harmless little green snake, sunning itself on a rock. He grabbed the snake before it could escape and dropped it into his pail. The boys had grinned at each other knowingly, and headed for the schoolhouse without a word.

The teacher had been startled when the two boys returned to class before being called. Assuming that it was time for class to begin, he had stepped outside to call the other students. While he was gone, James quietly slipped the snake under Elizabeth's papers, and F.W. put his frog behind a book on the teacher's desk. The schoolmaster should have suspected something was wrong when the two boys buried their heads in their schoolwork. But he did not.

The spring afternoon had begun peacefully. But with the warm sun shining, the temperature inside the school began to rise. F.W. peeked over his book, watching the teacher's desk. He nudged the boy beside him as the frog appeared in view. It was not long before the class was silently watching the frog perched on the edge of the teacher's desk. Swallowing their giggles, they pretended to be attentive when the teacher announced that it was time to recite the multiplication tables.

"Two times six is twelve," the pupils mumbled, "two times seven . . ." At that moment, Elizabeth's papers began mysteriously to creep across her desk. The frog took a mighty leap and landed at her feet, as the snake poked its head out from beneath her papers. Elizabeth screamed. The class went wild!

Part of the class dashed around the room trying to catch the frog, while the rest of the class crawled after the snake. The teacher shouted angrily. Benches were overturned. Papers fluttered in all directions. The Bonham girls clung to each other on their bench, avoiding a puddle of ink spilled from an overturned bottle. F.W. skidded across the room after his frog. He was too late. The frog vanished out the door. The little green snake managed to slither through James's fingers to disappear through a crack in the wall. When the excitement was over, the room was in a shambles. The teacher had looked like he might explode as he shouted, "School is dismissed! Go home — all of you!"

The teacher grabbed James's hand and stormed out the door, pulling the boy behind him. "Your father will hear of this, young man!"

"But . . . but . . . it was just a little old harmless snake. It wouldn't hurt anybody," James protested. "Besides, I'm sorry. I really am sorry."

The teacher had been in no mood to listen. When they reached the Bonham house, James never had a chance to say a word. The teacher kept shaking his finger angrily at James, "Spare the rod, spoil the child!"

Part of the class chased wildly around the schoolroom trying to catch the frog, while the rest of the class tried to get the snake.

James had never seen his father so angry, and his father certainly did not spare the rod. He sent James to bed without supper. James wondered if he would ever be able to sit on a chair again. He had never received such a spanking! James spent a long, fitful night trying to sleep on his stomach. He promised himself he would never play with another snake — or F.W. either.

After his father's death, James was different. Even the teacher had to admit that. James studied hard and almost never teased his sisters. With the change in James, the teacher regretted that he had turned in his resignation, but it was too late to reconsider. The schoolmaster figured that no job was worth trying to control a roomful of children with James around.

When the last day of the school year came, James waited until the other students had gone home. He wanted to talk to the teacher alone. "Sir," the boy's brown eyes lowered, studying the toe of his leather boots. "I'm sorry I have caused you so much trouble. I didn't mean to be bad. Honest."

The schoolmaster blinked and swallowed hard. "Son," he said, looking down at James. "I have watched you, and I must say you have changed since your father's death. If I could look into your future I would say that someday you could become a man of honor and dignity. A man that your family and Red Banks, South Carolina, would be proud of."

Neither James nor the teacher realized the truth of his prediction.


James and the new teacher hit it off from the start. Mr. Stewart had been warned that James would be a problem, but he found the boy to be a model student. By now, James stood head and shoulders above his classmates.

Everyone liked Mr. Stewart. The students were delighted to discover that he was not only a good teacher but also a wonderful storyteller. He added spice to their otherwise boring day of reading, writing, and arithmetic. His stories about Robert Fulton's steamboat — the *Orleans* — became their favorite.

"Teacher," William Travis said one afternoon, "tell us about that big boat."

Mr. Stewart never needed much encouragement to spin a yarn. "Students, you understand that I never saw one of Fulton's steamships." That was the way the teacher always started off his story. "I have been told that the *Orleans* was more than a hundred feet long and some twenty feet wide! The ship could go upstream, against the current of the Mississippi River, at the amazing speed of three miles an hour!" He paused.

"I'll bet my horse could go faster than that," James muttered to himself.

The teacher continued, "The *Orleans* was on her maiden voyage. It was around midnight, one night in 1811, when the captain pulled the whistle to let off steam. The noise was so great that the people on shore jumped out of their beds. They thought that the end of the world had come, or that the heavens were falling."

The children giggled at the descriptive picture.

William had a faraway look in his eyes. He muttered, "I wish I could have been there."

F.W. demanded loudly, "Where is the *Orleans* now?"

The teacher sighed and shrugged his shoulders. "I regret to say that the ship became entangled in brush and logs. The *Orleans* sprang a leak and sank to the bottom of the Mississippi River!"

James shook his head. "That's too bad."

Mr. Stewart nodded and went on with his story. "I understand that there is now a new vessel — the *Washington* — that can go round-trip from Louisville, Kentucky, to New Orleans in just thirty-five days!"

"Aw," F.W. argued, "my pa says a trip down the Mississippi River takes a couple of months."

"That was true, son, before they built the *Washington*."

"You just wait," James declared, straightening his shoulders proudly. "Someday I'm going to cross the Mississippi!"

William's blue-green eyes danced as he echoed James's statement. "Me too!"

The days and weeks passed quickly. Under the new teacher's direction, James learned to apply himself to his studies. Unlike his friend, William, he had never before been interested in schoolwork. Now things were different.

The first surprise came on the day that James outspelled his redheaded friend. He won the spelling bee by spelling "punishment" correctly. He repeated the victory the next day by spelling "misbehave." When he won the spelling contest on the third day, everyone, including the teacher, became excited. The class took turns rooting for one boy, and then the other. Finally, after several weeks, they knew that James was the new spelling champion of the school. Although he was the loser, William Travis was proud of James.

The spelling bees were just the beginning for James. He liked the feeling of being a winner. He took the highest honors in his other subjects before the year was over. Mr. Stewart's words of encouragement and praise made James feel ten feet tall.

Life in the Bonham home was changing too. Sarah's marriage to John Lipscomb was the social event of the season. For weeks before the occasion, the plantation was bustling with cleaning and sewing for the bride. After the wedding was over and things settled back to normal, James had to admit that he missed his older sister.

There were other changes too. James's oldest brother, Simeon, came home. He announced that he was moving to Alabama to open his own law offices. A short time later, James's other brother, Malachi, also left for Alabama. James could tell that his mother was very upset when his brothers left. With his brothers gone, James became the man of the Bonham plantation.

When they were not in school, James and his friend, William Travis, found time to go hunting and fishing. In later years, the two became expert horsemen and swordsmen. They took pride in those skills, but they were also careful of their manners and their speech.

One morning, before class started, William said, "Mr. Stewart, my father wanted me to tell you that we are moving."

"Moving?" James exclaimed in surprise. "Really moving? Where?"

"Alabama," William replied unhappily.

"I am sorry to hear that," the schoolmaster said. "When are you moving, William?"

"This is my last day at school. We are leaving Wednesday." William wiped a tear from his cheek with his sleeve. "Pa says I'll be going to a military school in Conechu County, Alabama."

"A military school?" James asked.

William wrinkled his freckled nose in disgust. "Doesn't that sound awful?"

James nodded slowly. "I sure will miss you. Who will go fishing with me?"

"I'll go," F.W. spoke up.

James did not bother to respond to F.W. He said, "William, will you write to me?"

"Sure, I'll be glad to. And maybe you can come visit me."

William Travis and his family packed their wagons and moved from South Carolina to Alabama. The two young men kept their promise. They exchanged many letters in the months and years that followed.


The year that his little brother, Milledge, entered school, James was like a mother hen with one little chick. His classmates quickly learned that they were not to tease Milledge. Twelve-year-old James was taller than the teacher, and almost as strong.

James had no friend his own age, so he turned to his younger brother for companionship. James surveyed the rice fields as Milledge sat behind him on his horse. James remembered riding with his father when he was small. He wanted his brother to have such memories too. James taught him things about running the plantation. He often asked Milledge questions.

"What are the plants in those wet beds, Milledge?"

"Rice seeds, and when they are ripe the workers will drain

off the water." Milledge would point to the tall shrubs with blue and white flowers. "And that is indigo. We sell that for money."

James nodded. "Some of that money will send me to college. But I won't go to college until I am seventeen."

"How old will I be?"

"In 1824 you will be eleven." James pulled up a clump of rice and inspected it carefully. "These plants do not look good. In fact, the whole field looks pretty bad."

A few years before his death, James's father had experimented with cotton and indigo plants. With the mild winters and long, warm Carolina summers, the plants had grown well at first. But hoards of insects had attacked the plants and stunted their growth. Without the captain there to supervise the plantation, the well-meaning workers had ignored the problem. The harvest had grown smaller and smaller. James's mother did what she could, but the more money she spent to improve the crops, the less they produced. Sophia Bonham found that running a large plantation was too big a job for an inexperienced woman.

The devoted workers did their best to help, but conditions worsened with each passing year. The house and buildings suffered from neglect. While the captain was alive, the Bonham stables had been renowned for their thoroughbred horses. Since his death, the stock had gradually declined along with the rest of the plantation.

The early 1820s brought many changes outside the settlement of Red Banks. Many people of Kentucky, Tennessee, and the Carolinas were moving west. Sophia wondered if she should sell her land and move to Alabama to be near her sons. The thought of leaving the plantation made her sad. Her people needed her and she needed them. She lay awake at nights worrying about what she should do. Sophia finally decided she could not move. Her heart was too entwined in each nook and corner of the old place. Everywhere she looked, she had memories of bygone days. She only wondered what the future would bring.

# 3

# Off to College

James absent-mindedly ran his fingers through his hair as he looked at his family. Now that the long-awaited day had finally arrived, he was filled with uncertainty. He did not feel right about going away to college and leaving his mother to run the plantation. There was so much work to do. James wanted to go to Columbia, and yet he felt that he should stay at home.

Watching his rambunctious brother was like looking at a mirror image of himself when he was eleven years old. James searched for words to say to Milledge. He finally placed his hand on the boy's shoulder and said, "I want you to take care of our sisters and Mama while I am away."

"With pleasure," the boy declared, with a devilish grin at Julia Ann and Elizabeth.

"Thanks, but I'll take care of myself!" Elizabeth's crinoline petticoats made a swishing noise as she stomped her foot. "I don't need you!"

"I want someone else to take care of me," Julia Ann giggled, "and it isn't Milledge Bonham!" James felt certain that she was thinking of the Bowie boy. He had been a regular visitor at the Bonham house until he left for college to study medicine.

A slight movement by the window caught James's attention. Jo-Jo, Milledge's old hound dog, peered around the curtain. James laughed at the forlorn look in his sad brown eyes. He declared, "Milledge, you can watch after Jo-Jo if the girls don't want you to take care of them. By the way — what is he doing in here? You know that mother doesn't allow that dog in the house. Jo-Jo knows it too. Get him out."

"Aw, he just wanted to tell you goodbye," Milledge grumbled, heading for the door. "Come on, Jo, you gotta go."

With a mournful look in his eyes and his long tail tucked between his legs, the dog crept out the door.

James looked down at his mother seriously. "Are you sure you will be all right? I really don't have to go to college this year. There is plenty for me to do right here."

A sweet smile softened his mother's face. "I've told you many times that your father wanted all of our children to have an education. He dreamed of you four boys becoming lawyers. His dream must come true."

"But it costs money to go to college. That money is needed here, Mother."

"Now don't you worry, James. This year's crops look good. We will make out just fine." The years since her husband's death had taken their toll on Sophia Bonham. She hated to admit how hard life had been. She had gradually allowed James to assume some of the responsibility. The thought of life without him made her feel old. Sophia struggled to hide her feelings. She was certain that James's keen sense of honor and loyalty would never let him leave her if he knew his mother's true feelings. "No, James, you will go to college. And so will Milledge, when he is older."

James noticed his mother's graying hair when he bent to kiss her cheek. She seemed so thin and frail. Yet James knew that his mother was a woman with undaunted courage. She was a great lady. James was determined to make her proud of him.

They walked outside, hand in hand. The workers of the plantation had gathered in front of the house to tell James goodbye. Most of them had known James since he was a baby. He was special. His going away to school was important to them, and they had talked of little else for weeks. It was a big occasion for them all.

The air was alive with excitement. Everyone tried to talk at once, to give James instructions or a word of encouragement. Thomas waited patiently beside the horse while James chatted with one after another. Finally, James took the reins from Thomas, shook his hand, and vaulted into the saddle. With a wave of his hand, James rode slowly through the crowd. He smiled at his thoughts. He felt like a knight from one of his favorite books. It seemed that he was riding to some unknown land to seek his fortune.

James had assured his mother that nothing could happen to him if he rode alone. His mother had finally agreed. It was only sixty miles to the town of Columbia on a well-traveled road.

After he left Red Banks, James was in unfamiliar country. He enjoyed seeing the plantations along the way. The sun was sinking in the west when he began thinking about a place to spend the night. Soon he came to the Midway Inn and decided to stop. After a good night's sleep and a hearty breakfast, he started out again. He had the road to himself that morning, except for a lone rider going in the opposite direction.

The trip was so uneventful, James wondered why his mother had been so nervous about him traveling alone. He remembered Mr. Stewart telling the class one day that there was no love like a mother's love. That was what made mothers so special. James smiled at the thought.

As he neared Columbia, James met other people going in his direction. He was surprised at the large number of houses and buildings. Compared to Red Banks, Columbia was huge! After he located the college, he tied his horse to a hitching post and walked to the office where he was to enroll. After completing an assortment of papers, James and the other new students were directed to their quarters. His baggage was already in his room. It had been sent by carriage, a few days before he left home. James busied himself by putting his things into place. When he finished, he decided to get acquainted with his classmates. It did not take him long to feel at home.

That evening the new students met with the dean of the college. He introduced them to the professors and answered their questions. Before the meeting was over, the dean gave a speech. He was a pleasant man, but he warned them that the college's rules of conduct were rigid and unwavering.

"We will not tolerate disobedience," the dean said. "Disobedience means punishment or dismissal from school. Remember — there are no exceptions. You young men are here to learn!"

The new students never doubted the dean for a moment. It was obvious that he meant what he said.

James and his classmates found that most of the professors were elderly men with dull, uninteresting voices. It was difficult to stay awake in class. James found that the hardest adjustment was getting used to the skimpy meals that were served in the dining room. The food was nothing like what he ate at home! He was not alone. Other students also complained about the food.

After class, James found time to go exploring. He visited the newly opened Medical University and the newest church in town — the Reformed Society of Israel. He went with a group of students to the theater to hear a musical program. During part of the program, the audience had an opportunity to sing. James liked to sing, so he visited the theater as often as possible.

There were a number of popular gathering places in town. James liked the Wild Stallion Inn the best. The owner, Mr. Wild, welcomed his customers with a glass of cider and seated them at one of the hand-hewn tables in the spacious dining room. The air was always filled with the tantalizing aroma of beef roasting on a spit in the huge fireplace.

The food at the inn was delicious. The menu consisted of roasted beef and chicken, baked beans and fresh hot bread directly from the ovens, crispy doughnuts, and apple pie served with hot tea or cider. Compared to the meals at school, this was a feast for James. The diners talked of politics and the weather. They exchanged a number of ideas before the night was over. The regular visitors to the inn knew that an evening would not be complete without one of the owner's exaggerated wild tales. Since Mr. Wild towered over most of his customers, few thought of disputing his word when he told one of his tall tales.

"That reminds me of a story." This was the innkeeper's signal that he was ready to spin one of his yarns.

"Story? Which one?"

"The one that my granddad used to tell about the snake hole."

The room always grew quiet when Mr. Wild started. The customers waited for him to begin. "Now, my old granddad was a farmer — and a good one at that. In the early days, life was hard. He worked from sunup to sundown. One spring the old fellow decided to clear the stumps and underbrush from one of his fields. He roped a yoke of oxen to a dead tree and yelled, 'Giddy-up!'"

Mr. Wild paused to light his pipe before continuing. "Of course, back then, you understand, a fellow always had to be ready for trouble. Granddad would strap a musket over one shoulder and an ax over the other, in case he needed them. Well, that day the oxen tugged and pulled. The earth finally let go around the base of that tree, and up it came! There was a big old hole where that tree had been. When my granddad leaned over and looked down in the hole, his blood ran cold!" Mr. Wild puffed on his pipe to let his words sink in.

"How come?"

"Yeah, what did he see?" someone whispered loudly.

"Well, I'll tell you what he saw. He saw more than a dozen rattlesnakes, wriggling this way and that, trying to get out of the hole. They were awful-looking creatures, fierce and poisonous! Why, some of them were bigger than your arm and more than six feet long!"

No one moved. The only sound was the crackle of the wood burning in the fireplace.

"My old granddad scarcely moved a muscle. He eased his ax into position under his left arm, lifted his gun with the other, and fired! His bullet blew the head off of one snake. Now . . ." Mr. Wild tilted his chair so he could look from face to face, "my granddad was as strong as an ox. So with a *whack! whack! whack! chop! chop!* — before those snakes could shake a rattle — my granddad had chopped off their heads with his ax! Not one of them varmints got away that day! What do you think of that?"

James thought it was a wild tale. However, in later years he remembered Mr. Wild's story when he had ideas of becoming a farmer.

In school, James studied a number of subjects, such as geography, history, and language. He and his fellow students did not find those subjects nearly as interesting as the beautiful girls of the town of Columbia. It was just as well that the school restricted the number of social events the students could attend, or the young men would have had little time for study.

The cold winter of that first year at school was followed by the warm days of spring. When those came, James had trouble keeping his mind on his books. He thought of leaving them to escape for a walk in the park, but he somehow managed to resist the idea. James continued to stay out of trouble until his senior year. That was the year that everything changed.

"It is wrong, I tell you. *Wrong!*" James's fist hit the table with a bang. His comrades, sitting around the dining room, blinked in surprise. James went on, "This school building is freezing. My feet and hands are numb right now! If they can't keep this place warm during a blizzard like this, they should not expect us to attend classes!"

"That's right, James."

"I agree," someone else said.

Encouraged by the comments from his fellow students, James's voice grew louder. "And look at this food. Why, back home we wouldn't feed this to the pigs! It certainly isn't fit for humans. It is awful!"

A student on his right cleared his throat and spoke up. "What you say is true, Bonham. The question is—what can we do about it? You know that we sent a committee to talk to the professors. They said that there was nothing they could do. They are cold and hungry too!"

Another young man joined in the conversation. "What is the solution? Your idea of wearing black for mourning didn't work, James. Do you have any other ideas?"

The room grew quiet. All eyes focused on the self-appointed spokesman, James Bonham. He crossed the room to the window and rubbed the frost from the glass to peer outside. The winter scene was one of fantastic beauty: tapering icy masses draped the tree branches, and the shrubs, like enormous balls of white cotton, protruded above the snow banks as far as the eye could see. James's tall body, clothed in somber black, blotted out the dim daylight filtering through the window pane. A lone, flickering candle on the fireplace mantle blended with the glow of the fire to offer light to the cold and dismal dining room.

James turned to face his classmates. He cried, "Throw the tea overboard!"

"The tea?" Tubby, the roundest student in the room, asked. "What ever do you mean, Bonham?"

"Don't you remember the Boston Tea Party, Tubby?"

The chubby fellow nodded his head, waiting for James to finish.

"We could take this . . ." James picked up the nearest bowl and held it over his head, "and throw it overboard!"

Tubby sprang to his feet with a laugh. "I understand. We take this . . . this . . . garbage," he seized the pewter vessel from the table, "and throw it!"

"Throw it where?" someone demanded.

"Anywhere! How about at the door?" Tubby aimed the dish in that direction.

"Stop!" James commanded. "You misunderstood my meaning. Violence will get us nowhere."

Several grumbled at the logic of James's statement and

James picked up a bowl and looked at his fellow students as he said, "We could throw this!"

watched him run his fingers through his hair. "Don't you see?" he said. "Whatever we do must be practical."

"I disagree." All heads turned to see who had spoken. James recognized the person at once. It was F.W. Pickens of Red Banks — the mischievous boy with the frog! F.W. continued, "I disagree with Bonham. The Tea Party was an act of violence, and yet it worked."

"He's right," one of the students agreed.

"I say we should throw this out." F.W. had a bowl full of mush in his hand as he started for the door. Others were right behind him.

Suddenly, above the confusion, a deep voice boomed from the stairway behind the students. "And what do you think you are doing?"

Awestruck at the turn of events, the group faced the college dean with fear and trembling. It had long been rumored that the man could mushroom to amazing size when he was angry. The bewildered students witnessed the transformation in their dean. His icy stare matched his voice. "I demand to know who started this commotion."

A number of telltale glances were cast in James's direction.

"And I want the names of those who participated; they will be punished!" The dean's words were loud and clear.

And punished they were. The incident resulted in most of the seniors of South Carolina College being dismissed. James Bonham and F.W. Pickens were among those who were expelled from school.

# 4

# Rallying to the Cause

James looked at the date and address on William Travis's latest letter: September 1835, San Felipe, Texas. He closed his eyes and thought of the many things that had happened since their school days in Red Banks. Over the years they had exchanged many letters and shared their dreams. Though miles apart, both had studied law and become lawyers. They were both interested in military affairs and craved excitement.

After his expulsion from college, James had managed to complete his education. In 1830 he was admitted to the bar and took up the practice of law in Pendleton, South Carolina. Three years later, there was talk of war when South Carolina nullified the tariff acts of the United States government. James organized and led an artillery battery in the Carolina militia. Later, when he was only twenty-five years old, he was promoted to the rank of lieutenant colonel. He served as aide to Governor James Hamilton of Carolina. Fortunately, the clouds of war had blown over and things settled back to normal. He was now practicing law in Montgomery, Alabama.

James sighed and looked back at the letter. William had described the raw, open beauty of Texas. He also wrote about her struggles. According to William, many Texans dreamed of independence from Mexico. This would offer an ambitious man like James an opportunity for excitement and glory.

James considered those words very carefully. He had read too many of William's letters to be easily swayed. James knew that one of his friend's strongest talents had always been that of writing letters which could stir the reader. During the three years he had been in Texas, William's messages had become more and more forceful. In this one he explained how he had been appointed colonel in the new army of Texas, after having served as commander of a scouting group. William's final words leaped from the pages: "Stirring times are afoot; come to Texas and take a hand in the affairs."

With those words racing through his head, James let the paper slip through his fingers. He shrugged his shoulders, mumbling to himself, "I guess there isn't much to keep me here in Alabama. The people here in Montgomery don't have much money to pay a lawyer."

Of course, James had to admit that he had experienced some interesting adventures. There was one that stood out above the others. On that occasion, James had been representing a very poor widow in court. The case should have been a simple one, but when the opposing lawyer did not show proper respect to the widow, James protested to the judge. But the judge — who, James discovered, had a personal grudge against the widow — did not agree, and James became angry. He proceeded to hit the other lawyer and threatened to pull the judge's nose! The judge was furious. He sentenced James to three months in jail for contempt of court. James did not mind. He received no money for that case, but he did become the town's hero. Many of the women in town came to visit him while he was in jail. They saw to it that he was well supplied with delicious things to eat.

James chuckled softly at the memory and took his empty money pouch from his pocket. "Well," he muttered to himself, "I guess it's my fault that this is empty. I am just too tenderhearted to demand large fees like the other lawyers. One thing is certain — there isn't enough money here to take me far! I'll go back to Red Banks and settle up my affairs. That will give me a chance to tell Mama and Milledge goodbye before I leave for Texas."

Once James made up his mind to join William, it did not take him long to close his law office and head for home. His mother was delighted to have him back. She hoped he would stay. When James explained he was moving to Texas, she seemed to understand that it was something he felt that he had to do. While he was home, James sold some of his valuables to raise money for his trip.

When it came time for him to leave, his mother said, "Son, are you certain that you want to go to Texas?"

"Yes, Mother."

"James, I haven't much to give you, but I want to give you something I have treasured. I want you to have my horse, Belle. I know you will be good to her. She is a good horse."

James was deeply touched by the gift. He knew that Belle was his mother's pride and joy. Belle was saddled and waiting for James when he was ready to leave. When the moment of departure came, James kissed his mother and squeezed her hand. He sighed deeply, "Mama, all I can say is thank you. You have been good to me and I love you. I promise to take good care of Belle."

—With a flurry of last-minute instructions and fond farewells, James mounted the beautiful cream-colored horse and headed west. He recalled the day that he had left for college, feeling like a knight from the olden days. He wondered if he would find his fortune in Texas.

It was almost dark when James came to an inn, where he decided to stop for the night. While he was eating, James overheard a discussion about a group of men in Alabama who were forming a militia to go to Texas. After asking some questions, James learned that the group — the Mobile Grays — was leaving from Mobile, Alabama, before the week was over. He decided to leave for Alabama at once, in hopes of catching the group before they left. He rode swiftly along the way and arrived in Mobile just in time. The Mobile Grays were happy to have James travel with them.

A touch of fall was in the air that hazy morning in mid-October, 1835, when the party rode out of Mobile. Mile after mile they traveled, pausing only long enough for the men to stretch their legs and to rest their horses. They rode up mountains and down into valleys, through rivers and across dry creek beds. The countryside along the way was ablaze with color. James had never seen so many colors of leaves on the various kinds of trees. During the days, the temperature was pleasant, but after the sun went down, a penetrating chill crept in. The men always looked forward to finding a place to camp for the night. When they stopped, they built a roaring fire and cooked something to eat. The fire offered them warmth and protection from wild animals. After some sleep and a hurried breakfast, the group was on its way again before daybreak. They crossed the border of Texas at a settlement called Nacogdoches and then turned toward the southwest.

One evening they made camp beside a stream. They were gathering wood for the fire when they heard a dog barking. The Mobile Grays grabbed their guns and waited. Two men and a boy, with his dog, came out of the woods toward them.

"Howdy," the older man said. "Where you from?"

"We're the Grays from Mobile, Alabama. Who are you? And where are you going?" James asked.

"My name's Wilkinson, and me and my family are going back to Tennessee. We didn't come to Texas to fight a war. Or haven't you heard of the latest trouble with Mexico?" When James and the others shook their heads, the man went on. "Well, in September, the Mexican government sent soldiers to Gonzales — that's where we're from — demanding our cannon. That cannon had been given to the town as protection from the Indians. The folks of Gonzales refused to give up the cannon. The womenfolk made a 'Come and Take It' flag and the men chased the Mexican soldiers back to San Antonio. And that's the way things stood the last we heard. We packed our wagons and left. I don't want my boys gettin' killed in a war."

One of the Grays spoke up. "Who is leading those men from Gonzales?"

"The last we heard, Stephen Austin was — and it wasn't just men from Gonzales. There were some from the other settlements too. Mark my word, there's going to be trouble. That old Santa Anna — he's the president of Mexico, you know — isn't gathering a big army for nothing. Well, me and my boys had better get going. We're camped just down the way a bit. Where did you boys say you were heading?"

The men in the Mobile Grays looked at each other, waiting for someone to speak up. A deep-voiced man finally replied, "We just might be heading for San Antonio!"

After their visitors had departed, the group discussed the situation. They finally decided to ride to the nearest town, San Felipe, in order to buy supplies and ammunition and learn more about what was happening in Texas.

A slow drizzle was falling when they rode into San Felipe. In one of his letters, William had explained that the town of San Felipe was founded by Stephen Austin. By 1824, Austin had brought three hundred families from the United States. They had settled along the Brazos and Colorado rivers. They had faced Indians, floods, and sickness to claim their land grants of 4,428 acres each.

After the six-week journey, James and the Grays, and their horses, were tired. The first thing they wanted was something to eat, and then a warm place to sleep. James left the others at the Whiteside Hotel and went out to find a blacksmith. Belle needed a shoe replaced. He found the blacksmith shop without much trouble and made arrangements for the smith to shoe his horse. Then he said, "Mister, do you know a man named William Travis?"

The blacksmith wiped his forehead with his arm and looked at James. His brown eyes twinkled, and a friendly grin spread across his face. "Travis? Buck Travis?"

James nodded.

"Everybody knows Buck. He's the recruiting officer." With a critical eye, the blacksmith studied James's tall, muscular build and rugged face. "Texas needs men like you. Are you gonna join our fight for freedom?"

"I might."

"You ought to find Buck in his law office down the street. That's where he usually is." The smith turned to his hammer and anvil to finish beating the molten metal into a horseshoe.

James walked past several weather-beaten buildings before he came to one with the word "Lawyer" written above the entrance. He opened the door and quietly stepped inside. Although it had been a number of years since the Travis family had moved from Red Banks, James recognized William at once by his bright red hair. James folded his arms and leaned against the door, studying the man who was sitting at a table working on some papers. He cleared his throat. "Mister, can you tell me where I can find a friend?"

William looked up in surprise. As he recognized his visitor, he leaped to his feet exclaiming, "James Bonham!"

For the next hour they relived boyhood days. William asked questions about his friends back in South Carolina. He wanted to hear about everyone. Finally, he asked, "Did you receive my last letter, James?"

"I did. That is why I'm here."

"You got here just in time. Mark my word — the year 1836 will bring war to Texas!"

"Why do you say that, William?"

"Most of the men have already loaded their guns. They came to Texas pledging to be law-abiding Mexican citizens. They have made settlements out of a wilderness. It took sweat — sometimes blood — to cut and notch enough cedar logs to build a house without nails or equipment. These settlers have faced not just hard work, but savage Indians, wild animals, and starvation. Now they feel that this land is theirs. Most of them are willing to die for it."

"I can understand that, but what is wrong with the Mexican government?"

William's blue eyes flashed while he talked. "Many things. Mexico got her independence from Spain back in 1821. Since then, things have changed. The new president, General

Antonio López de Santa Anna, has become a powerful dictator with grand ideas. He isn't following the laws laid down by the Constitution of 1824. Instead, he has made up his own laws to get the people under his control." William paused to catch his breath. "Did you hear about what happened at Gonzales?"

"Yes, I heard that the men of Gonzales chased the Mexican soldiers back to San Antonio. How far is San Antonio from here?"

"It is about 175 miles southwest of San Felipe. The Mexican soldiers under General Cos used the old mission, called the Alamo, as a fort."

"Who is your leader, William?"

"Sam Houston is now commander of our Army of the People, or Texans, as we call ourselves."

James looked surprised. "Houston? The Sam Houston who fought in the Creek Indian War of 1812 with Andrew Jackson?"

William nodded. "The same. Folks around here sometimes call him the Raven. That was the name that the Cherokees gave Houston when he lived with them. The general is a man of few words, but I trust him. James, when you are ready to join us I will be glad to write a letter of introduction for you. With your previous experience, you will be made an officer right away."

"Where is Stephen Austin? I understood he was in charge."

"Austin was commander-in-chief until he was relieved of his command at San Antonio. He has gone to the States, to appeal for money and more men. Austin is a fine fellow. Unfortunately, he has not been in good health since his return from Mexico. Freedom for Texas is very important to him."

"What is wrong with him?"

William shrugged his shoulders. "My guess is that those two years in Santa Anna's jail affected his lungs. Austin has a terrible cough."

"Two years in jail? What had he done?"

William clinched his fist in indignation. "Nothing! He went to Mexico to discuss the problems in Texas, and he ended up in prison. I'll tell you, Santa Anna has made many enemies!"

James looked surprised. "Enemies?"

"Why, even Austin, who trusted the man, calls Santa Anna an unprincipled dictator! Some of the *Tejanos* in San Antonio are afraid of Santa Anna and his political aims. They are ready to fight with us, for freedom for Texas!"

"Is that right?"

"Yes, there are solid citizens like Erasmo Seguin and his son, Juan, of San Antonio. Juan Seguin fought with us against General Cos during the Siege of Bexar. When General Cos surrendered on December 10, Juan rode with us as we escorted Cos and his Mexican soldiers down to the Rio Grande. According to the treaty they were not to return. But mark my word, the trouble is not over yet."

James stared at his well-worn boots. Finally, with a shrug of his shoulders, he said, "I guess I have heard about all I need to, William. Where do I join up?"

A few days later, James presented William's letter of introduction to Sam Houston. It stated that James Butler Bonham was volunteering his service, without conditions, in the struggle of Texas. James was accepted immediately and was commissioned a lieutenant in the cavalry.

Weeks later, James recalled William's warning that there would be trouble. News came that General Santa Anna and some seven thousand Mexican soldiers were seeking revenge for Cos's defeat at San Antonio. The troops were marching toward the Rio Grande. There was little doubt that Santa Anna was preparing for all-out war. He would take no prisoners.

# 5

# The Alamo

James looked at the scene below. How quickly time had passed. It was now the last week of February 1836. He shook his head, thinking of the people he had met and the stories he had heard since he arrived in San Antonio in January.

He had heard many things about the Alamo before he ever reached San Antonio. He learned that the Franciscan priests had built this old church back in the early 1700s. It was here that the priests had tried to Christianize the Indians. But, with the passing of time, the Indians had returned to their old ways. The mission had been abandoned and had fallen into disrepair. From where James was standing, on the roof of the Alamo, he could see the three-acre compound and the buildings which now served as barracks for the Texans. The whole area below was enclosed by thick rock walls about twelve feet high. Obviously, time had weakened those walls. There was a gaping hole along the north end. It was clear that the mission was never intended to be used as a fort.

"One thing is certain," James remarked to the man standing near him on the roof, "this place was never built to be a fortress against the Mexican army!"

"You're right," Almeron Dickinson replied.

"I've been gone for five days. Tell me what has happened while I was in Goliad, trying to get Colonel Fannin's help," James said.

"Well, while you were gone those five days, we worked on these cannons that General Cos left behind after the Siege of Bexar back in December." Dickinson chuckled, "Micajah Autry has been helping me. I'll make him into a blacksmith yet."

Autry smiled. "You're trying, anyway."

"What else happened?" James asked.

"Early yesterday morning, our lookout in San Fernando Church spotted Santa Anna's men marching toward town. If I live to be a hundred I'll never forget that February 23!" Dickinson declared. "When the bells of the church started ringing, the women and children went wild, screaming, 'They're coming — Santa Anna's coming!'"

"Travis gave the order for everyone to get back inside the walls of the Alamo. Some Mexican families ran in. Others ran in the opposite direction!" Autry said. "By the way, Bonham, did you pass John Smith and Doc Sutherland when you rode back yesterday?"

James shook his head. "No."

Dickinson scratched his head thoughtfully. "You should have. Colonel Travis sent them to Gonzales for help. You know, I think Santa Anna has a mighty peculiar way of fighting. We get to shooting good and he decides to stop! Of course, maybe it's just as well. It gives our boys a chance to patch the holes in the walls before the next round of shooting starts. In fact, since things are quiet right now, I reckon I'll go check on my wife and baby." Dickinson headed down the dirt ramp which led through the church below.

Autry sighed and returned to cleaning the cannon. "I'm glad that my family is back home. I'd hate to have them here."

James watched the men in the courtyard below. Some were repairing a break in the south wall. Others were reinforcing the embankments of dirt which served as platforms for the

Mexican cannons that the Texans were using. James shaded his eyes to look to the west, past the row of wooden shacks some distance from town.

"Say, Autry, what is that red flag flying from that church tower away over yonder?"

"That's old Santa Anna's warning to us that no prisoners will be taken — no quarter, he calls it. Our water supply comes from the river twisting around the town. It runs over there by the east wall. If his troops should shut off that water supply, we will be in trouble. That well down there in the yard isn't half finished."

Watching the flurry of activity along the walls, James thought of the strange turn of events that had brought him to this place. He had met the famous Jim Bowie while serving as William's assistant recruiting officer in San Felipe. James had heard many stories about Jim Bowie's knife and his fights. Bowie's search for a lost gold mine had taken him to San Antonio. There he had met and married the beautiful Ursula de Veramendi. They were blessed with two fine children. Jim's business affairs often took him away from San Antonio and his family. While he was away, Ursula frequently visited her friends in Mexico. During one of those trips an epidemic of cholera broke out. Many people — including Ursula, her children, and her parents — contracted the dreaded disease and died. When Bowie learned of their deaths, he was grief-stricken. His friends said that Bowie was never the same after that. There was even talk that Bowie had joined the Texans in hopes of being killed. These thoughts and many others raced through James Bonham's head as he stood on the roof of the Alamo. He suddenly realized that Micajah Autry was speaking to him.

"Bonham, how long have you been here in San Antonio?"

"It was the middle of January when I rode in with Colonel Bowie's unit. General Sam Houston had sent us with orders to blow up the Alamo."

"Really?"

James nodded. "But Commander James Neill and Bowie felt that Santa Anna should be delayed here at the Alamo.

They hoped to give Houston time to recruit more men for Texas. So, Houston's orders were not obeyed."

"Where do you think Neill is now?"

"Home, I suppose. When Colonel Travis arrived during the first week in February, Neill gave up his command. I understand that there was sickness in Neill's family, so he went home. With him gone, Travis and Bowie were both in charge. I think Bowie was wise to turn over his command to Travis. Bowie is a sick man." James did not say that some thought Bowie's sickness was from pneumonia or tuberculosis. Everyone knew he had collapsed one morning and had to be carried to the hospital. They also knew that Col. William Barret Travis was facing an army of thousands, with only some 150 men under his command.

"You know, it's mighty reassuring to look down there and see Davy Crockett and his men from Tennessee along that south wall," Autry said.

"It certainly is. Colonel Travis posted them there because of that weak spot in the wall. Say, do you think the wild tales about Davy fighting bears and wild animals are true?"

Autry shrugged his shoulders. "Who knows? I've seen him use that old rifle he calls Betsy. He is a real sharp-shooter, that's for sure! And he's some fiddle player too."

James chuckled softly, "Yes, but that bagpipe of John McGregor's is something else!"

Their conversation was interrupted by a flurry of shells from Santa Anna's camp. Almeron Dickinson raced up the ramp to rejoin his comrades on the roof. Then, as abruptly as it had started, the Mexican guns were silenced. James and the other Texans did not like the sudden outbursts of fighting. They found that the enemy's tactics were hard on their nerves.

"Santa Anna's men moved closer during the night," Dickinson remarked, "but it didn't seem to improve their aim, did it? They make plenty of racket, but none of our men have been hit yet."

James studied Capt. Almeron Dickinson while he was talking to him. Dickinson was a likable fellow. James felt sure that he was concerned about his wife, Susanna, and their little

Angelina. They, and a number of Mexican women and children, were in the church below. James was glad that he had never married. If he had a wife, he would not want her in the Alamo — not now.

Shortly after dark, on the evening of February 24, the Alamo gate was opened for Capt. Albert Martin to ride out through the enemy lines. Martin carried in his saddlebag Colonel Travis's second plea for help. James had seen the letter addressed to the "People of Texas and all Americans in the world." It stated that not one man had been lost during the twenty-four-hour attack. Travis had also written: "I shall never surrender or retreat... VICTORY OR DEATH!"

After Albert Martin rode off toward Gonzales, the Mexican soldiers started shooting again. Travis sent word to his men to hold their fire until reinforcements arrived. Their supply of ammunition was very low. James knew that Santa Anna had received additional soldiers. He could see them moving closer and closer. Without ammunition, how could the Texans stop them? James was not the only one concerned.

Down by the south wall, Davy Crockett complained, "I don't know about you fellows, but I'd rather be out there fighting in the open. Never did like being cooped up behind walls like these. This isn't my way of fighting."

James agreed. He felt like a fly caught in a spider's web. He did not like the feeling, and the weather did not help. Before dawn, a cold wind with a freezing rain dampened their spirits. To make matters worse, the firewood was almost gone.

"Boys, I don't know about you, but I'm cold," Crockett said. "I reckon the only solution to the problem is to tear down those shacks over yonder. Who will go fetch us some wood? You'll be safe — we'll keep you covered." He waited for an answer.

Several men volunteered. They slipped out the south gate and ran to the empty huts along the river bank. After quickly knocking down the huts, they returned with arms full of wood. They then carried the wood to their companions who were huddled in different spots around the wall. The Texans soon had several fires going. Blankets were stretched above the fires to keep the rain from putting them out.

James crouched near a cannon, on the church roof, staring at his comrades stationed around the courtyard below. The men were a motley group, dressed in moccasins and buckskin breeches and jackets. Wide-brimmed hats protected their faces from the blowing wind. Few of the men had been born in Texas. Some were from England, Scotland, and Germany. Others were from the states of Virginia, Alabama, Tennessee, Pennsylvania, New Jersey, and elsewhere. Although they came from different places, they all had a common goal: to fight for freedom and justice and Texas.

James knew that most of the men had no previous military training. They were farmers, lawyers, doctors, hunters, and blacksmiths. They also varied in age. William Malone was barely eighteen years old and Robert Moore was fifty-five. Some of the men were short, like twenty-four-year-old Henry Warnell, who had been a jockey. A few, like Davy Crockett, William Travis, and James Bonham, stood head and shoulders above the crowd. Regardless of their differences in age and appearance, the men were loyal to Texas.

# 6

# A Glimmer of Hope

It was late the next evening when five men entered the room that served as Colonel Travis's office. He looked from one to another — Juan Seguin, Davy Crockett, Almeron Dickinson, Green Jameson, and James Bonham — before he spoke.

"I have called this meeting to discuss our most serious problem. Gentlemen, we *must* have reinforcements!" he paused. The sound of the Mexican cannons broke the silence. Travis cleared his throat and continued. "I have written another message; this one is to Gonzales. I feel you should hear part of it:

> *It will be impossible for us to keep them out much longer. If they overpower us, we fall a sacrifice at the shrine of our country, and we hope posterity and our country will do our memory justice. Give me help, oh my country!"*

No one spoke. Each man was deep in his own thoughts. Dickinson swallowed hard. A picture of his pretty wife and baby floated before his eyes. He said, "Sir, if you are sending that message to Gonzales, I am sure we'll get help."

"I hope you are right, Dickinson." Travis looked from one to another slowly. "The question is — who will volunteer to take this message? You realize, of course, that there is now danger in trying to leave. That danger grows worse each day. Santa Anna's soldiers have us surrounded."

The men were silent.

Juan Seguin spoke up. "Sir, there is a chance that I could get out. If the enemy should stop me, I would answer them in Spanish. Hopefully, they would think that I am one of their soldiers. I am willing to try, but I must borrow a horse if I go."

The men in the room knew that Juan was right. He was the only one who could speak Spanish. Most of the others knew only a few words of the language.

"Besides," Captain Seguin went on proudly, "I know this country. I am a *Tejano*."

Travis's shoulders slumped as he said, "All right, Juan. Take one of your men with you, and borrow Jim Bowie's horse to ride."

Hours later, Juan Seguin and Antonio Cruz y Arocho slipped past the enemy's guns to begin the seventy-mile ride to Gonzales.

"William, today's the twenty-seventh and there is still no word of what is happening in the rest of Texas." James yawned, adding, "I could use a good night's sleep." Santa Anna's continuous bombardment and unending false attacks made sleep impossible.

"We could all use some sleep. But I sent for you, James, because I need your help. If anyone can get Fannin to come to our aid, it is you!" William looked tired and worried.

"What can I do?"

"James, you are my friend. We are like brothers. I hate to, but I must ask you to make a second trip to Goliad. You — and you alone — have the persuasive powers to make Colonel Fannin send us help. I know he could send at least three hundred men — perhaps more. Just think what they would mean to us! Why, even two hundred would more than double our present number. If Fannin sends them we would have a chance. As it is . . ." Travis did not finish.

"What would you have me tell Colonel Fannin?"

Travis slumped wearily in his chair. His voice sounded flat when he spoke. "Stress two things. First, let him know that while Santa Anna has received reinforcements, none have been sent to us. Yet, three of our messengers have ridden out of these walls. Tell Fannin that we are still able to come and go — with precautions."

James chuckled softly. "Crockett's boys had no trouble slipping out to tear down those shacks for firewood the other night."

A half smile crossed William's face. "Yes, and they cleared that area on the north and east so that we can watch for snipers. You stress to Fannin that his men will still be able to get into our gates."

"If they try," James grumbled under his breath.

"That is your job, my friend. You *make* Fannin try. Understand?"

James nodded and headed for the door with his hat in his hands.

"Wait . . . there is one more thing. When you return, James, tie something white around your hat brim. We will be watching for you. And another thing. Listen for our cannon signal. We will fire at dawn and dusk each day to let you know we are still here." Colonel Travis's face was grim. "Bring us help, James."

"I will try." James's words faded in the darkness.

A short time later, under the cloak of night, James rode Belle past the Mexican soldiers. He wondered if the sentries were sleeping at their posts as he sped by. After he had cleared their camp, James relaxed his grip on the reins and patted his horse's neck.

"Belle, old girl, we are on an important mission. We have a hundred and eighty miles ahead of us to Goliad and back. So we will just keep a steady pace." The mare whinnied softly as if she understood.

Mile after mile slipped past. The rosy glow of morning

streaked across the eastern sky as James paused at a shallow creek for Belle to get a drink. They did not tarry long.

Hours later, James rode into the camp at Goliad. The sentry led him to a group of men. James recognized one of them as Col. James Fannin. "Captain Bonham reporting, sir," James said as he slid from his horse.

The colonel smiled. "Sit down, Bonham. You look tired. My men will see to your horse. Someone bring us some coffee."

James studied the officer's boyish face as he took the coffee. He recalled several of the stories he had heard of him: Fannin's brief stay at West Point and his efforts to resign his post at Goliad when trouble had started with Santa Anna. It was whispered that James Fannin had trouble making an important decision.

Considering those facts, Bonham decided not to mince words. He went right to the purpose of his visit. "Colonel Travis sent me for reinforcements. Santa Anna has the Alamo surrounded! We must have help *now!*"

The colonel listened politely. Then, much to James's surprise, he agreed to send help. Colonel Fannin said, "In a case like that, I will gladly send Travis some of my men." He ordered his captain to load supplies on the wagons. James waited impatiently as they loaded the supplies and ammunition. The men gathered up their gear and started out. They had gone only a short distance when they stopped. Three of the supply wagons had broken down. While the wagons were being repaired, some of the oxen wandered away. Without the oxen, the wagons could not go on. James was furious when Colonel Fannin ordered his group to return to camp. He informed James that he had decided not to go to San Antonio after all.

James Bonham tried to conceal his anger. "Sir," he said unhappily as he remounted his horse. "I am sure that somewhere in Texas there are courageous, loyal men willing to fight for freedom." Under his breath he muttered, "But apparently, not here!" James turned his horse toward the town of Gonzales.

Seventy miles away at the Alamo, the hours of Saturday

and Sunday passed slowly. Noise from Santa Anna's guns was unending. Finally, in the early morning hours on the first day of March, the lookout shouted, "Somebody's coming!" He raised his gun and fired.

"Stop shooting, you fool! We're reinforcements from Gonzales," John W. Smith shouted. When the gates flew open, the small band of thirty-two men rode into the Alamo.

The weary Texans around the walls of the mission came to life. With help arriving, their gloom was turned to joy. They rekindled the fires, and a celebration of corn and beef was soon under way. Davy Crockett played a tune on his fiddle while John McGregor blew on his bagpipes. The men danced and celebrated until after dawn.

Almeron Dickinson stayed at his post on the roof of the church and watched the scene below. After the noise died down, he leaned over the edge and shouted, "It is mighty good to see you fellows from Gonzales. I told Colonel Travis he could count on you to come. Say, if we count my wife, Susanna, and little Angelina, there are some forty of us here now from Gonzales!"

"Captain Dickinson is right. We are proud of you for coming to our aid," Colonel Travis said. "In fact, even though we are short of ammunition, we are going to celebrate your coming by firing the cannons." He pointed toward the town of San Antonio. "Dickinson, see if you can hit one of those buildings over yonder. Are you ready?"

A forceful whoop was the answer.

"All right. Cannoneers ready — fire in the hole!"

BOOM!

When the smoke cleared, Dickinson squinted his eyes to see if he hit the mark. As he watched, a cloud of rubble burst into the air. "We hit it, sir! We hit that house!"

"Whoopee!"

"Good work, Dickinson. See if you can do it again. Ready — fire!"

Colonel Travis's words faded away as someone yelled, "It missed . . . but look! There's old Santa Anna himself!"

All heads turned. The general's brightly colored uniform

shimmered in the morning light. The Texans fired at the arrogant rider prancing his white horse. It was obvious that the general knew he was safe.

"Save your bullets, men," Davy Crockett shouted in disgust. "He's too far away for you to hit. And he knows it. Just wait — we'll get our chance before long."

# 7

# Darkness Creeps In

James Bonham stared at the women crowded around him. "You say you sent only thirty-two men?" His tone betrayed his disappointment.

"Mister, Gonzales isn't very big and those thirty-two were more than Fannin sent." The woman hurried on, not waiting for James's reply. "In fact, three of our boys were hardly dry behind the ears!"

"That's a fact. They were only sixteen-year-olds!"

The first woman went on talking. "They left here on February 27 and should be in the Alamo by now. Isn't that right, Sam?"

Sam Highsmith nodded his head. "That's right. They've been gone three days now. Say, young fellow, you and that horse of yours look plumb tuckered out. You had better just stay here. There is nothing that you can do all by yourself."

James's eyebrows rose in surprise. "Stay here? You don't understand. My friends are in the Alamo. Colonel Travis needs me. But my horse and I could sure use something to eat."

The women bustled around, seeing to James's needs. When he finished eating, he checked the stirrups on his saddle. Sam Highsmith shook his head. "Son, I tell you you're making a mistake. You ought to stay right here in Gonzales. We'll find you a place to stay."

"No, thank you, sir," James muttered as he remounted his horse. With a wave of his hand he was off again.

Sam Highsmith watched the rider until he vanished from view. He mumbled softly, "Now that fellow is a brave Texan. That's for sure."

James discovered that he had to stop every few miles to rest. He and Belle were both exhausted. He tried in vain to shake off the feeling of doom that had settled in his heart. James felt like a moth drawn to a flame — he had to return to the Alamo, regardless of the cost. He imagined that he could hear his mother saying, "Nothing is impossible with faith." His belief in honor and loyalty to his friends and Texas erased his fears.

It was almost noon on Thursday, March 3, when James approached the Alamo. It was obvious from the shell-scarred walls that it had been under heavy assault during his five-day absence. For one brief moment he questioned the logic of making a dash through the enemy lines. But valor — that intangible bravery deep within his soul — forced him to go on.

He whispered softly into his horse's ear. "Old girl, we have made it this far, but we're taking a chance riding further. I'll tie this handkerchief around my hat. When we near the gate, I will bend over your neck, Indian style." He gently stroked the horse's lathered neck. "You have been a faithful friend, Belle. Are you ready? Let's go!" Off they dashed.

The startled soldiers in Santa Anna's camp stared in disbelief at the cream-colored horse racing toward — not from — the south wall. The lookout on the wall of the Alamo saw the rider, too, and ordered the gate to be opened. James Bonham and his horse sped through the opening as bullets whizzed past. In his mad dash James never felt the bullet which grazed his forehead nor the one that hit his horse, until Belle sank to

Bullets whizzed past James as his horse sped toward the open gate.

the ground under him. He was too dazed at first to realize what was wrong.

The men rushed to help James to his feet. He ignored the blood trickling slowly down his cheek. He could only stare at Belle. With her help he had twice carried messages out of the Alamo for Colonel Travis. Belle had given her life in the process. His mother's beloved horse was dead.

It was Davy Crockett who put his arm around James to take him to Colonel Travis. He took James into the office and returned to his post. The semidarkness of the room eased the sadness in James's heart. He sighed loudly. "Well, Fannin isn't coming!"

"Is not coming?"

James's somber face matched his words. "That's right. Fannin said to tell you that they started out but his wagons broke down. They turned back."

Travis stood speechless. His fists were clinched in anger as he paced back and forth across the small room. "Very well," he declared. "So be it! We will fight this battle without Fannin. History will someday bear witness to our determination to stop the enemy."

Bonham's head throbbed from his wound. His body ached from his hours in the saddle. He suddenly felt numb.

"You look exhausted, my friend. Lie down for a while. I have another letter to write. I must let the men know that someone will ride out tonight if they want to write to their families. This may be our last messenger to leave."

James thought of Belle and her heroic efforts as he drifted off to sleep.

Hours later, he was awakened by the sound of shooting. "Go back to sleep," William said, looking up from the papers on his desk. "That is our diversion to help John Smith get through the enemy's lines with our messages."

"Where is Smith going?" James mumbled sleepily.

"To Gonzales and on to San Felipe — I hope."

The March skies were black with smoke from Santa Anna's guns. The Texans watched the shells hit the stone walls of the Alamo, again and again. The next day — Saturday, March

5 — a bitter north wind brought an ominous feeling of suspense.

The men inside the walls of the old mission clustered together, watching the enemy prepare for a final assault. Santa Anna's soldiers carried ladders and pushed cannons into place as they spread their circle in all directions. By evening they were in position and settled for the night.

Meanwhile, at their posts around the walls, the Texans shivered and tried to stay awake. The minutes and hours crept by slowly. The temperature went lower and lower. The weary men dreamed of hot coffee, knowing that the supply had long since disappeared. One by one the men slumped at their stations. They were too tired to care. The war of nerves had taken its toll. They had no idea what the morrow would bring.

James Bonham felt that he had just closed his eyes when the sound of running feet reached his ears. He rubbed his eyes to stare into the early morning darkness as he mumbled to himself, "What is happening?"

From the muffled voices in the distance and the thud of feet, there seemed little doubt that Santa Anna had chosen this Sunday to make his final assault. The enemy drums rolled their signal of attack and were followed by the roar of cannons. James knew that the battle to the death had begun. There was no fear in him. Whatever happened, he and the other Texans were ready to face it with dauntless courage.

James and his comrades stationed on the church roof loaded their cannons. The ground below shook as thousands of Mexican soldiers ran toward the Alamo from every direction. The pale morning light made it difficult to see the shadowy figures, until it was too late to shoot with accuracy. With the coming of dawn, the Texans sent a barrage of well-aimed bullets into the oncoming troops. The air was soon filled with the deafening noise of battle. Cannons boomed amid screams and moans.

In the fury of battle James caught sight of his friend, William Barret Travis, standing on the north wall. He heard Wil-

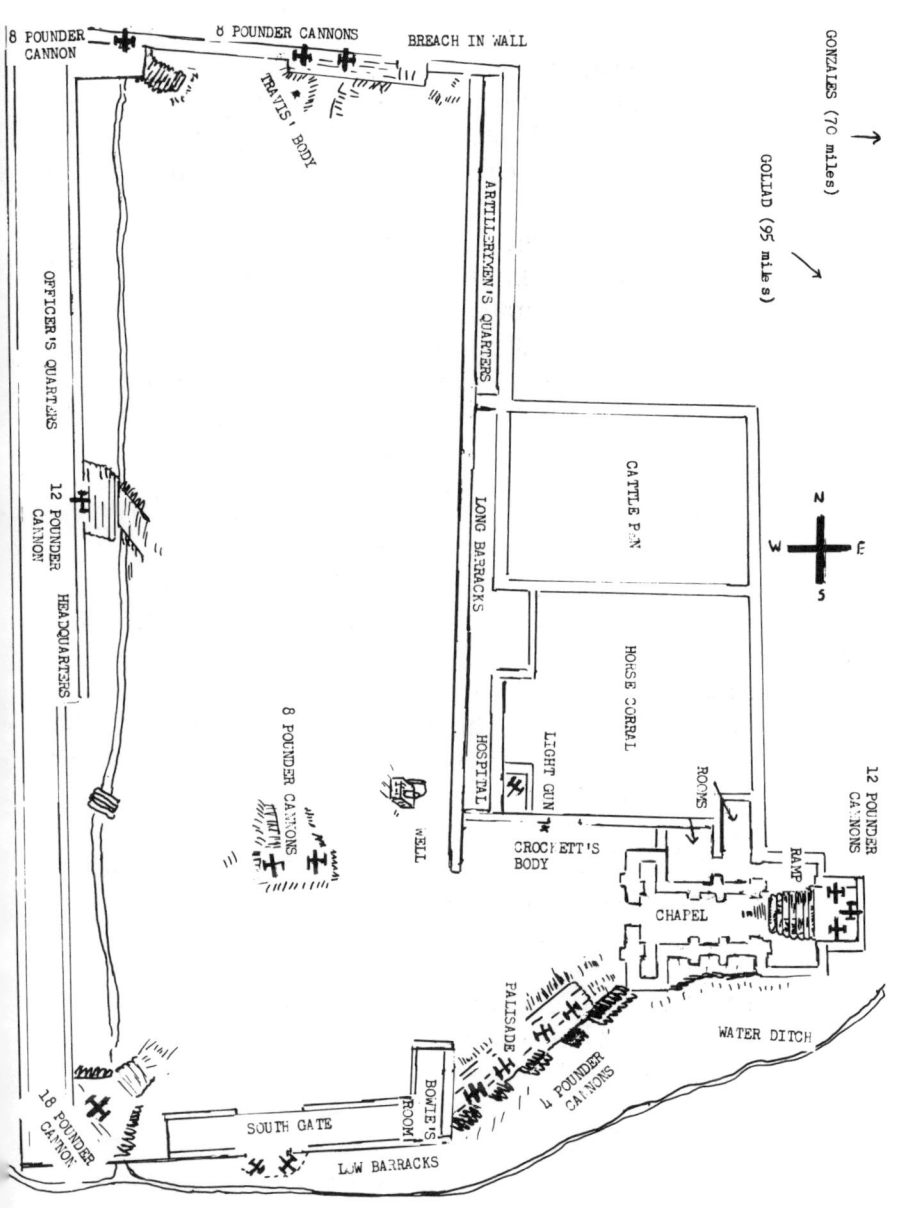

Alamo positions in the final battle.

liam shout, "Here they come, give 'em . . ." Travis's words stopped abruptly. James saw his friend stagger and slump to the ground. A bullet had hit him in the forehead. Before James could leave his post, someone yelled, "Colonel Travis is dead! Stay at your stations — and keep shooting!"

The angry Texans fought like demons. Endless columns of Mexican soldiers rushed forward through the smoky haze. Cannonball after cannonball crashed into the weak spot in the north wall. Rocks in the weakened wall began to crumble, leaving a gaping hole. Santa Anna's men poured through the hole like water through a broken dam. Once inside the compound, the Mexican soldiers fanned out in all directions. One group battered down the door to the barracks and ran inside. They found Jim Bowie waiting for them, with his long knife in one hand and his gun in the other.

"Long live Texas!" Bowie whispered from his sick bed. The soldiers answered with a hail of bullets. Jim Bowie did not die alone. He took a number of Santa Anna's men with him.

Meanwhile, the Texans fighting around the walls had no time to reload their guns. They were forced to swing their guns like clubs, in hand-to-hand combat with the enemy. Santa Anna's men kept pouring into the grounds from every direction.

The cannoneers atop the barracks' roof fired and reloaded, and fired again. Many of the Mexican soldiers sank to the ground without ever knowing what hit them.

On the roof of the Alamo, James Bonham, Almeron Dickinson, and others did their best. For each soldier they hit, three more appeared to take his place. The choking clouds of gunpowder smoke lifted for one brief minute. James caught a glimpse of Crockett and his men near the south wall. Using knives and their guns as clubs, the fearless men from Tennessee lashed out again and again against the slashing bayonets of the enemy. Crockett's proud volunteers rallied close together as they fought for their lives. James reloaded his cannon. As he fired he muttered, "Danger truly makes men valiant."

Before James could fire again, someone shouted, "They got Davy!" James stared at the spot where Crockett had been only seconds before. Davy Crockett lay dead near a mound of lifeless bodies. A furry coonskin cap lay near his feet. Davy's musket was still clutched in his hand.

James wasted no time grieving. He had troubles of his own. The Mexican soldiers were storming up the roof.

"James, they . . ." Almeron Dickinson did not finish his words as the bullet hit him. He fell dead beside James.

A wild-eyed Mexican soldier, crazed by battle, raced toward James. The Texan saw him coming and, with a forceful swing of his rifle butt, crushed the soldier's skull. James spun around. The cold steel of a bayonet pierced his heart. With his last breath, James Butler Bonham drove his knife into the soldier's chest. With that final deed, he slumped over his cannon — dead.

The noise of battle gradually faded until the guns were silent. All of the gallant Texans had fallen one by one: William Travis, James Bonham, Antonio Fuentes, Davy Crockett, Gregorio Esparza, Micajah Autry, Almeron Dickinson, and the other brave defenders of the Alamo. After thirteen days, the battle was over. The Alamo had fallen, but the memory of those brave men would never die.

# Epilogue

The final battle of the Texas Revolution occurred on April 21, 1836, at San Jacinto. There, Gen. Sam Houston's Texans defeated Santa Anna and his Mexican army in a battle which lasted less than twenty minutes.

The valiant men of the Alamo had not died in vain. Their names were etched in the hearts of fellow Texans forever.

# Bibliography

**Juvenile**
Lyman, Nancy A. *The Colony of South Carolina.* New York: Watts Publishers, 1975.
Tunis, Edwin. *Colonial Living.* New York: Thomas Crowell Company, 1957.
———. *Frontier Living.* Cleveland: World Publishers, 1961.

**Adult**
Bonham, M. L. "Bonham, James Butler," *Southwestern Historical Quarterly* 35 (1933).
Meyers, John. *The Alamo.* Lincoln: University of Nebraska Press, 1975.
Smithwick, Noah. *The Evolution of a State.* Austin: University of Texas Press, 1983.
Time-Life Books, eds. *The Texans.* Text by David Nevin. New York: *Time-Life* Books, 1975.
Webb, Walter Prescott et al., eds. *The Handbook of Texas.* Austin: Texas State Historical Association, 1952.

**Newspaper Clippings**
"Birthplace of a Hero of the Alamo." *Saluda [South Carolina] Standard,* August 14, 1941.
"Bonham House Ruined." *Waco News-Tribune,* January 16, 1959.
"Bonham Left Alamo Twice, But Returned." *San Antonio Express,* August 20, 1955.
Eargle, L. B. "Old Bonham House." *Saluda [South Carolina] Standard,* December 18, 1958.
Elliott, Keith. "Good Man." *San Antonio Light,* April 23, 1979.

## ABOUT THE AUTHOR

Rita Kerr is a graduate of San Antonio College and Trinity University. She is a member of a number of organizations, including Texas Library Association, Daughters of the American Revolution, Daughters of the War of 1812, and Daughters of the Texas Revolution. Rita was a teacher in the San Antonio Independent School District for a number of years. Upon retirement she started a new career as a writer of historical books for children.

Much of the author's time is now devoted to lecturing about early Texas. Dressed in pioneer clothing, she discusses her exhibit of artifacts and pictures. Rita endeavors to make history come alive for her audiences. Five of her ancestors came to Texas in 1824 and were among Stephen F. Austin's "Old Three Hundred."

| DATE | ISSUED TO |
|---|---|
| SEP 2 5 2006 | |
| OCT 2 3 2006 | |
| NOV 2 2 2006 | |
| DEC 0 5 2006 | |

3986

B
BON

Kerr, Rita.

Texas cavalier : the story of James Butler Bonham.

RIO HONDO JUNIOR HIGH SCHOOL LIBRARY

**RIO HONDO SECONDARY SCH LIBS**

RIO HONDO JUNIOR HIGH SCHOOL LIBRARY

998446 00931 55480C 05907F